How
Billy Brown
Saved
the Queen

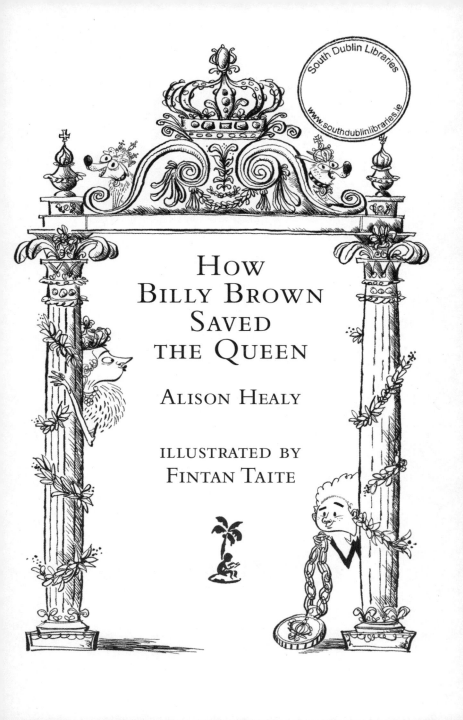

How Billy Brown Saved the Queen

ALISON HEALY

ILLUSTRATED BY
FINTAN TAITE

HOW BILLY BROWN SAVED THE QUEEN

First published in 2018 by
Little Island Books
7 Kenilworth Park
Dublin 6W
Ireland

ISBN: 978-1-910411-95-7

A British Library Cataloguing in Publication record for this book is available from the British Library

Typeset by Catherine Gaffney

Printed in Poland by Drukarnia Skleniarz

Little Island receives financial assistance from the Arts Council/An Chomhairle Ealaíon and the Arts Council of Northern Ireland

10 9 8 7 6 5 4 3 2 1

For my family

1

Billy Brown was quite surprised to find himself standing in the Queen's bedroom. It was 4.12 AM on a Friday morning and she was eating an egg. He didn't know what was more surprising: the fact that Queen Alicia was eating a boiled egg in bed or the fact that he was there to witness it. *This is definitely going to be a much better day than yesterday*, he said confidently to himself.

The day before had, without doubt, been the worst day in the short life of Billy Brown. He had come last in the Sports Day race. Again. He never won anything, even though he tried so very hard. He'd gone into training before this Sports Day. Billy ran around the garden 27 times until he got dizzy and nearly fell over. Then he touched his toes 17 times. And just to be sure of victory, he did 12½ star jumps. After all that effort, he was certain he would win the race. Everyone would crowd around him, slapping him on the shoulder, saying things like, 'You're our secret weapon. Who knew you could run that fast?'

But when the whistle blew and the race started, everyone passed him out without even trying. It was like he was running in a big pool of syrup. Even the boy on crutches hopped past him just before the finish line. That was the worst part of it. No, there was something even worse. It was when he burst into tears in front of everyone. Billy blamed his mother for that. She saw how sad he looked after the race and came up to give him a hug.

It's a well-known fact that mothers have the power to make you cry just by hugging you if they catch you at a weak moment. Of course, the tears came. A nine-year-old like Billy might get away with that if they were small tears that could be blinked away. Unfortunately for Billy Brown, the tears were big and snotty and noisy.

Billy made a strange gulping noise that he had never heard before. He actually thought the noise was coming from his mother until he realised he was doing it. It felt like a million pairs of eyes were staring at him. Of course Billy realised that this was not mathematically possible because there were just 302 children in the school, but it still felt that way. It was so bad that his mother asked the teacher if she could take him home before the prize-giving.

'All I want to do is to win one thing,' he cried that night. Yes, he was still crying, 6¼ hours later. 'Why can't I get a prize just once?'

'Oh, Billy, you're good at lots of things,' Mum said, hugging his little red head close to her.

'No, I'm not. When I drew a picture of an alien you thought it was Gran. When I sang at the concert a small child burst into tears.'

That was true. Billy had an unusual singing voice that sometimes scared nervous children and small furry animals.

'And when I played the tin whistle at Daddy's party, Aunt Annie squeezed her glass so tight it shattered in her hand.'

Sadly, that was also true. Aunt Annie spent seven hours in the accident and emergency department and needed 12 stitches.

'Remember how I told you that it was a very, very thin glass, Billy? So easily shattered,' Mum said, patting him on the back. She didn't tell him that it was the last glass in an extremely valuable set that had been passed down from her great-great-great-grandmother. She didn't tell him that she had gone into the bathroom and quietly banged her head against the wall because she was planning to sell the glass so that she could repair the hole in the roof.

Sometimes it's nice to see that little patch of daylight coming through the hole in the ceiling. It's like bringing the outdoors indoors, Mum told herself as she stood in line to pay Aunt Annie's hospital bill.

But Mum didn't say any of this to Billy. Instead she said: 'Well, I know something you're brilliant at.'

Billy's big blue eyes lit up. 'What, what is it? Javelin? Ping-pong? Karate?'

'School,' she said. 'You're brilliant at school, especially maths.'

His face fell. 'Who wants to be good at school? I'll tell you who. Absolutely nobody. That's who. And who wants to be nobody? Definitely not me.'

Mum knew exactly what he meant because she was just like Billy when she was a child. It seemed like everyone in her class had had a talent for something except her. The only time she was the best was when she got ten out of ten in her spelling tests. She had so many gold stars she could have opened a shop selling only gold stars. But it definitely wasn't as good as winning a race or an art competition.

After Billy had gone to sleep, Mum turned on the news and saw something that made her spill her tea all over the sofa. Buster the dog got very excited too and started running around the room yelping. The newsreader was saying that Queen Alicia was very, very cross. She couldn't understand how dividing a number by a fraction made it bigger.

'One understands that dividing something makes it smaller so one cannot understand how dividing it by a fraction makes it bigger,' she said in her lovely, tinkly, posh voice. 'Not one person in my empire can tell one why. It is most frustrating.'

This was a very big news story because no one wanted to see Queen Alicia upset. She was the most popular ruler for approximately 564 years. In fact, a recent survey found that she was the world's number-one queen, taking 99.8 per cent of the vote. When she went into the garden, birds perched on her head. When she walked on the beach, dolphins did synchronised backflips for her. Her eyes were bluer than the bluest sky and her long wavy hair cascaded down her back like a river of rich caramel.

No one in the empire had ever seen the Queen make even the tiniest frown but now she looked almost sad. The biggest brains in the country had spent 976 days trying to explain the sum to her but she still didn't understand.

'One is dreadfully sorry to have to inform the empire that a small gloom will hang over the rest of one's life because of this. One won't be sad all the time, of course. But just as one is sitting down to a glorious 18-course banquet, one will suddenly remember the maths problem and a bit of joy will slip away,' Her Majesty said.

'Or one will receive a beautiful bouquet of flowers from a child and will be so happy until it occurs to one that the very same child probably knows the answer to one's conundrum.'

Mum woke Billy up immediately, or even a bit sooner. He had just fallen into a brilliant dream where he was running the race again but this time he had grown wings and had soared so high in the sky that he felt a tickle in his belly. He was about to come back down to earth and win the race when Mum came running into his room. She was acting very strangely.

'Why does a number get bigger, instead of smaller, when you divide it by a fraction?' she asked.

'Ah, that's easy,' said Billy. And without opening his eyes he launched into an explanation that made Mum's eyes glaze over at first but then the fog lifted and she understood.

'Now can I go back to my dream and win this race for once?' Billy asked his mother, his eyes still squeezed shut.

'No, you can dream of winning all the races in the world later. But first you have to get dressed,' she said. 'We're going to the palace and you're going to tell Queen Alicia exactly what you've just told me.'

The palace! It felt like the middle of the night and the palace was hours away. Was Mum having a dream? But no, she was fully alert. So alert that she told him to brush his teeth first. Which of course he didn't do. But he wet his toothbrush in case she checked.

2

Billy fell asleep as soon as he put on his seatbelt, and he had another very happy dream about Sports Day. This time he won the hurdles, the egg and spoon race, the Parents' Race and the Teachers' Race. When you're that good, you have to try everything.

Mum had no time for dreams as she was driving the car. Instead she imagined how Billy would impress the Queen so much that she would invite them to her next garden party. Mum had picked out the outfit and hat she would wear by the time they reached the golden gates of the palace. She just wasn't 100 per cent sure about the shoes.

They had driven non-stop for six hours when they reached the palace. When Mum got out of the car her legs felt like two wobbly jellies. Possibly strawberry or raspberry flavour.

The palace was only four hours away but they had spent 123 minutes driving around in continuous circles on 17 different roundabouts. You see, Mum had a habit of getting lost. Billy felt like he was on a carnival ride at one point and almost asked for candy floss.

It was 4 AM when they arrived at the palace and everything was in darkness. Mum approached the man in the box beside the gate and explained how Billy could help to solve Queen Alicia's very, very tricky sum. He was immediately interested because he had watched 249 of the country's greatest brains coming into the palace day after day to explain the sum. Every one of them had left with a very red face. He had watched the Queen's smile getting a tiny bit smaller every day. Could this freckle-faced nine-year-old boy really turn her frown upside-down? It was worth a shot.

The man in the box rang the bright red phone which must only be used for major emergencies such as earthquakes, volcanos or a worldwide shortage of tiaras. This was an emergency to equal any of those, he told himself as he dialled the number.

The Queen's lady servant was asleep and so was the servant of the lady servant. But happily the servant of the servant of the lady servant was wide awake. She stayed awake every single night to be prepared for exactly such an emergency.

The servant of the servant of the lady servant was thrilled to hear the red phone ringing. She had just been wondering about her all-night vigils and was thinking of introducing a 30-minute nap every second night. The arrival of the brainy red-headed boy proved exactly why her all-night vigils were essential.

She woke the servant of the lady servant. She in turn woke the Queen's lady servant.

'It is truly a national emergency,' the Queen's lady servant said in a most important voice.

She was so excited that she took Mum and Billy straight to the royal bedroom. 'Ma'am,' she said to Queen Alicia. 'Apologies for the disturbance but it is a mathematical emergency. This child says he can solve your very, very tricky sum.'

The Queen was sitting up in bed eating a boiled egg. In a gold egg cup. With a teeny, tiny golden spoon. The tiniest little golden egg cosy lay on her diamond-encrusted tray. She always got up at 4 AM because she wanted to be awake before her subjects. 'Stop,' she said, raising her hand.

Mum and Billy stood at the door, petrified. After all, the Queen could order their beheading if she felt like it. And they were standing in her bedroom at approximately 4.12 AM. Just then Billy remembered that he hadn't even brushed his teeth. He was also pretty sure that he had a hole in his right sock. He stretched his big toe and felt no sock. If the Queen knew! His cheeks went red.

Mum had a horrific thought. She had absolutely no idea how to approach the Queen. Were you supposed to bow? Or do that funny curtsy thing? Did she read somewhere that you have to walk backwards curtsying when you leave her presence? Mum froze to the spot while thinking about her options. Then she decided to try a bit of everything so she bowed low and repeated an awkward curtsy three times.

'Is your back giving you trouble again?' asked Billy with concern, as she nearly toppled over.

The Queen didn't even notice Mum's efforts. She had beckoned her lady servant, who lifted her gold crown from her little golden locker and carefully placed it over her cascading curls.

The Queen smiled. 'Now you may approach.'

Billy stood looking at the Queen sitting up in her bed with a crown on her head and wondered if this was the strangest dream he'd ever had. He decided that he would not pinch himself just yet as he was really enjoying it. Then he realised the Queen was looking at him expectantly.

'Well, young man? Do please tell one why a number gets bigger when you divide it by a fraction.'

'That's easy, Your Honourable Ladyness,' said Billy. He knew 'Your Ladyship' didn't sound right but he had slept so much on the way to the palace that he hadn't had time to ask his mother how to address a queen.

He started to explain the sum, while Mum tried to memorise everything about the royal bedroom. She knew that she would tell this story about 4768 times and she wanted to make sure that she had the details absolutely right. Ideally she should take a photograph but that might trigger a national security alert so she ruled that out.

The Queen was wearing the finest silk nightdress, edged with the softest white fur. The daintiest high-heeled white fur slippers Mum had ever seen sat on a gold rug beside her bed. Size five slippers, Mum estimated. *The same size as my own.* Guessing the size of people's feet was one of Mum's party tricks. She didn't tell people she had worked in a shoe shop for two years.

The Queen's bed had a high canopy that sparkled with hundreds of tiny diamonds. It was just what Mum had imagined a royal bedroom should look like. A little part of her had feared that it would be an ordinary bedroom with flat-pack furniture and a faded dressing gown covered in make-up stains.

She was happy to note that the Queen's dressing gown was pink cashmere and was entirely covered in pearls of different sizes. The bottom of the gown was covered in big pearls and they grew smaller as they reached the top of the gown. *You couldn't throw that into the washing machine,* Mum thought. Well, she *thought* that she thought it but she actually said it out loud by mistake.

The Queen looked at her, frowning. 'What is this "washing machine" you speak of?' she asked. 'Should one purchase one?'

But before Mum could answer, the servant of the lady servant had wheeled in a gold-framed whiteboard and the Queen immediately switched her attention to that. Mum was relieved because she had been opening and closing her mouth like a fish, wondering if she should tell Her Majesty about the 24-hour sale on washing machines in Electric City. She was very hazy on the rules surrounding royal encounters. Why, oh why, hadn't she bought that book she had seen in the shop last week? *Everything You Need to Know about Speaking to the Queen while Standing in her Bedroom* had been reduced to €1. Mum was going to buy it but then she saw *The Essential Guide to Surviv-*

ing a Zombie Apocalypse and she decided that would be a more practical read. After all, when would she ever find herself in the Queen's bedroom? Whereas a zombie apocalypse was always just around the corner.

Within seconds Billy had covered the whiteboard in numbers and equations and was looking at the Queen to see if she was keeping up. The Queen was almost frowning. Time stood still. All Billy could hear was the ticking of the gold clock on the bedside locker.

'Well?' he said impatiently. 'Do you get it now, or will I explain it again? I don't mind doing it again if you're a bit slow at maths.'

3

The Queen stared at the board and narrowed her eyes. Then she clapped her hands with delight.

'Now one understands,' she said. 'One truly does. You are an absolutely fabulous boy. No fewer than 249 of the country's best mathematicians spent 976 long and very boring days trying to explain that sum to one. They brought fat books with more than 500 pages in each of them. They did PowerPoint presentations that went on for half the day. One could hear one's jaw creaking from yawning so much. They held conference calls with Nobel Prize winners. They Skyped the smartest person in the world. One believes he's a British astrophysicist. And yet they all failed to do what you have done in two and a half minutes.'

Billy beamed with happiness and Mum thought her heart would burst with pride for her boy.

'I'm very surprised that you didn't learn this at school,' said Billy. 'Or do trainee queens go to school at all? Ms Rodahan taught us how to do that sum when we were very young.'

'Sadly one cannot go to a regular school when one is preparing to be a queen,' Her Majesty told Billy. 'We had private classes at the palace. Your queen got top marks for walking with dignity while wearing a crown. Appearing to look interested while listening to an incredibly boring speech was a most enjoyable class. One was less successful in the study of subsection 2 (f, g and h) of the constitution. That made one's head hurt. Yes, basic mathematics was taught but if one didn't understand anything, the tutor just said, "Don't worry about it. You'll never need to know about multiplication when you are ruling the empire."'

'That's a pity,' said Billy. 'You probably should have had Ms Rodahan. She'd never let you away with that. Now what about the multiplication of fractions? I can run through it with you if you like, after you've eaten that egg.'

'One is most grateful for your kind offer but I think that's quite enough mathematics for today,' said Queen Alicia, smiling.

'From where does he get the mathematical skills?' she said, turning to Mum. 'Is it from you or the boy's father?'

'Definitely his father,' said Mum. 'I'm numerically illiterate but extremely good at spelling. If you ever have a spelling emergency, please call me.'

Just then Mum realised that they had completely forgotten about Billy's father, Benjy. He had been in bed when she woke Billy. Perhaps he was still asleep, not knowing that his wife and child were in the Queen's bedroom talking about mathematics and washing machines. She had better ring him before he reported their kidnapping. Mum asked the Queen if it was okay to contact Benjy to let him know where they were. 'Why, of course,' said Queen Alicia. 'One shall ask one's lady servant to alert your butler at once.' Mum and Billy laughed inwardly at the idea of a butler standing to attention in 10 Rockfort Avenue but they were careful not to let the laughter bubble out onto their faces. 'I'll just send him a text so I don't disturb his nocturnal slumber,' said Mum, trying to sound posh.

She started composing the strangest message of her entire life: *Gone to palace. Billy helping Queen with tricky sum. She has a gold egg cup. Don't forget to let the dog out.*

While Mum was preparing to wake Dad with the most extraordinary text, the Queen told her lady servant to fetch the extra-special box. It was such a big box it had to be wheeled in. It had a collection of the most magnificent gold medals Billy had ever seen. The Queen picked out the biggest, shiniest medal.

'This is for you because you are truly the best at sums in my whole empire.'

Billy was so excited he thought he might float right out through the golden window. Finally, he had won a medal. And what a medal! It was so heavy he couldn't even wear it around his neck. He was so happy he forgot himself and gave the Queen a big, warm hug.

Her servants froze. Mum gulped. She definitely remembered a rule about never, ever touching the Queen. But then Queen Alicia straightened up and beamed. 'Thank you, my boy. That was most refreshing. One doesn't get hugs very often. You have made my day and it's still only 4.25 AM.'

Everyone let out a big sigh of relief. Then Billy high-fived the Queen and everyone sucked in their breath again. But Queen Alicia was still smiling. Mum took Billy's hand and pulled him towards the door in case he did something else inappropriate. She still wasn't sure if you were allowed to turn your back on the Queen, so she reversed out the door, curtsying and waving like a mad thing. The Queen had the biggest smile on her face and Mum thought she saw a tear glistening in her eye. What an interesting woman!

To this day, Billy doesn't remember the journey home. That's because he fell asleep as soon as the golden gates closed behind them. His dreams were even better on the way home.

Mum looked at Billy in the mirror, as he clutched the medal and smiled in his sleep. 'Yes, Billy, you are the best, and you have the world's biggest gold medal to prove it. I always knew it.'

Billy's smile widened and he let out a big snore.

You may think that was the end of Billy's adventure with the Queen but you would be very wrong. It was only the start.

4

Billy awoke to find the sun streaming into the car. His face was stuck to the window with dribble and he had such a bad taste in his mouth that he wondered if he had mistakenly eaten a badger for breakfast. Then he looked down. There it was, nestling in his lap. No, not a badger. It was the biggest, shiniest gold medal he had ever seen. It sat there twinkling in the Friday morning sun. It wasn't a dream after all.

'Well, sleepy head,' said Mum as she pulled into the drive and turned off the ignition, 'we're a bit late for school and you get your summer holidays today. Do you want to go in at all?'

'Do I what?' said Billy. 'This is going to be the best school day of my whole life. But first I need breakfast.' He jumped out of the car and

ran inside. Buster was jumping up and down in the kitchen and Dad was sitting at the table reading the paper.

'The wanderers have returned,' he said, before the medal caught his eye. 'Mum said it was big but she didn't say it was the size of a dinner plate. A very big dinner plate. I have breakfast ready, so you sit down and tell me everything.'

He started to put the sausages on a plate. 'You wouldn't get that in the palace, would you?' said Dad, as he handed Billy the plate.

'Ha, no!' laughed Billy, not knowing that his father would use this expression 7678 times in the next 12 months. It wouldn't take much encouragement. Dad might put a nice dinner on the table. 'You wouldn't get that in the palace, would you?' he'd ask Billy. Or he might get a good parking space at the super-market. 'You wouldn't get that in the palace, would you?' Dad would say. Or he might mow the lawn neatly. 'You wouldn't get that in the palace, now, would you?' he'd say proudly. Usually it made no sense at all, but Dad didn't mind.

'What about work, Benjy?' Mum asked. 'Are you not going in today?'

'Well, it's not every day your son gets a gold medal from the world's top queen so I rang work and said I had to take a royal day. It's a little-known fact that everyone is allowed to take two royal days a year, to allow for royal engagements.'

In between mouthfuls of sausage and eggs, Billy told the story of the Queen and the very, very tricky sum. Mum filled in the bits about the royal bedroom and the gold egg cosy and fancy slippers. It was the best breakfast they had ever had. Then Billy put on his uniform, put the medal in the purple box the Queen's lady servant had given him, and off they went to school.

Billy was right. It was the best school day ever in the worldwide history of top school days. He actually found himself feeling sorry for Lightning Luke Bolt, the boy who won the Sports Day race. Billy sat beside him and couldn't help noticing that Lightning Luke was wearing his Sports Day gold medal and it looked like a one cent coin beside Billy's enormous gold disc.

Billy's teacher told him to go around to every classroom and show off the medal. All the teachers wanted to bite it to see if it was real gold but he didn't want the teachers' enormous teeth marks all over it so he politely said, 'No, thank you very much, the Queen does not allow it,' when they asked. Then everyone got sweets because it was the summer holidays.

And, even better, Dad arrived to collect him from school in case the medal got damaged on the way home. Well, that's what he said, but Billy knew Dad just wanted to show off in front of the other parents. He had even put on a tie in case anyone took a photo.

All the neighbours ran out to see the medal when Billy arrived home. Then the aunties and uncles arrived and soon Billy had a headache from people rubbing his head and telling him what a great lad he was. The only bad part was that he had to explain the maths problem about 354 times because everyone wanted to hear how he had explained it to Queen Alicia.

Then the biggest surprise of all happened. A big black car pulled up outside and a chauffeur with a peaked cap got out and opened the back door. Who was it, but the Queen's lady servant? And she was standing outside their house on 10 Rockfort Avenue.

'Goodness gracious!' said Mum. 'What will we give her to eat? We haven't a thing in the house except three and a half digestive biscuits and a packet of stale Cream Crackers.'

But the lady servant had no interest in digestive biscuits or even Cream Crackers. She was holding a cream envelope etched with gold. It was an invitation to Queen Alicia's Summer Garden Party. 'Her Royal Highness requested that I hand deliver it personally,' she said, and Billy realised that she also had a very posh voice. He hadn't noticed her voice in the palace because everyone there had a posh voice. Even the Queen's little fluffy dogs

barked in a posh way. A 'yup, yup' instead of a 'yap, yap'.

And the purple parrot had a particularly posh chirrup.

Mum nearly knocked over the lady servant in her effort to grab the invitation from her gloved hand.

'Ahem,' said the lady servant. 'The invitation is to your son Billy and two guests.'

Mum blushed a furious red and handed the invitation to Billy. 'If you don't invite me and your father,' she hissed into his ear, 'we'll put you up for adoption.' And then she kissed his head and gave that weird tinkly laugh she made when she was extremely nervous.

Dad came out to see what all the commotion was about and insisted that the lady servant come in. She refused a few times but in the end she said she would like to use the facilities before they got back on the road.

'The facilities,' said Dad, looking mystified. 'Which facility in particular are you thinking about?' He was trying to think of the facilities that a Queen's servant would want. The computer? The wi-fi code? The microwave?

'Why, the lavatory of course,' she said and blushed a little. It is an unspoken rule that Queen Alicia's staff must never say words like loo, toilet or lavatory out loud. If they do, a bluebird loses a feather in the Amazon rainforest.

Then it was Dad's turn to blush as Mum showed the lady servant to the bathroom. Mum was secretly very pleased that she had just replaced the everyday towel with the fancy one. She had also lit the very expensive candle that she normally saved for very extremely special occasions.

The lady servant actually stayed for a long time, even though she kept saying, 'I really must go home.' She spent ages looking at the medal and even asked Billy for a tour of the house.

Billy wasn't especially good at giving the tour. He just stood at the top of the stairs and pointed, saying: 'There's the bathroom, there's my room, Mum and Dad's room, the spare room – which is also the junk room.'

But the lady servant seemed to be very interested in everything and asked Billy approximately 67 questions about his family and the neighbours. When she finally decided to leave, she pressed a card into Billy's hand.

'Here is my number. If you ever have need of help, just call me, day or night.'

Billy looked down at the card. The lady servant's name was Gwendoline Penelope Remmington-Bakhurst. 'That must have been very tricky when you were learning how to spell your name,' he said.

'Not at all, my darling boy. I sat beside Maxima Alexandra Olympia Haffenden von Tranten Zinnenburg. She was ten before she could spell her entire name, poor girl. It took up two lines in her copybook, for goodness' sake. Mine was quite short really.'

What a day! Billy was almost glad when the last visitor left. It was Aunt Annie, waving her still-bandaged hand.

'Now, Billy, give me the medal and we'll hide it away under my pillow for safe-keeping until we figure out what to do with it,' Mum said.

'Ha, ha, very funny, Mum,' Billy answered. 'You know I don't have it.'

Mum gave him a strange look. 'Benjy, do you have the medal?' she said in a wobbly voice.

Dad shouted, 'No,' as he came back into the house.

The three of them looked at each other and the colour drained from their faces. Where was the medal? Billy felt like a cold, dead hand had just grabbed his heart and squeezed it until he could not breathe. Approximately 39 people had passed through the house since he came home from school and now his extremely special and very valuable medal was missing. Was the best day of his life about to turn into the worst day ever?

5

'Seriously, Benjy, stop messing around,' Mum said. 'It's not funny. Give us the medal.'

But Billy knew Dad was not messing because he didn't have his messing face on. He really did not have the medal. Within minutes they had turned the house upside-down. Every cushion had been lifted. Every bed stripped of its sheets. Mum prised Buster's mouth open in case he was hiding the medal, even though it would have been physically impossible because the medal was bigger than the dog's head. Billy pointed this out but Mum said now was not the time to be going all scientific on her.

Dad searched in the parrot's cage and behind the cat's ears. Billy found himself looking up the shower nozzle. Things were getting desperate. Where on earth was the medal? Even the purple padded box was missing.

Mum made Billy retrace his steps. When was the last time he'd seen it? But Billy couldn't remember. The evening was such a haze.

'There's only one thing for it,' said Dad. 'We have to ring everyone who was here and ask them if they have it.'

Mum objected immediately. 'That would be beyond embarrassing, to admit that the medal is missing. Not to mind insulting. You're basically accusing them of stealing the medal. We cannot let anyone know what's happened. Ever. EVER.'

But Dad said he would be discreet about it. He'd say something like, 'By any chance did that old medal of Billy's fall into your handbag this evening? Or maybe your big pocket?'

'No!' Mum screeched. 'That's even worse.'

One part of Billy agreed with Mum and the other part agreed with Dad. He would be mortified if he had to tell people he had lost the Queen's medal. But then he would hate to think that someone had taken it. The only one he had ever won. And he was hardly likely to ever win another.

Then he spotted something on the side-board. The lady servant's business card. She had told Billy to ring if he ever needed help. Maybe now was the time.

But Mum hesitated. 'How can we tell the palace we lost the medal within 24 hours of receiving it?' she said. 'We are going to look like such fools.'

Dad agreed. 'Let's all have a cup of tea and think about our next move. No point in rushing into anything.' He went off to put on the kettle and Billy snuck out the back door with the phone and dialled the palace.

A dreadfully posh voice answered the phone. Billy took a deep breath. 'Is that Gwendoline Penelope Remmington-Bakhurst?' he said. You need a very big breath to say a name like that.

'Is that Billy?' said a voice full of surprise. 'How wonderful to hear your darling voice so soon again.'

He explained the disappearance of the medal as quickly as he could, while being very careful not to put any blame on himself. He wasn't quite sure how it happened, but one thing led to another and by the time he had ended the call, the lady servant was making arrangements for the Queen to travel to 10 Rockfort Avenue first thing in the morning to help with the search.

Mum and Dad were sitting at the kitchen table clinging on to mugs of tea like they were lifeboats in the middle of the ocean when Billy came in to break the news. Dad was using the mug with the Queen's face on it. Billy tried to imagine the Queen sitting beside them eating a digestive biscuit. It was no good. He could not picture it.

'Why are you scrunching up your face, Billy?' Mum asked. He backed out of the room slowly and, just before he closed the door behind him, he stuck his head back into the kitchen.

'I rang the lady servant. The Queen is coming in the morning to help search for the medal. We need to clear out the spare room.' And then he ran up the stairs as fast as he could and hid under his bed.

6

Mum stood up and immediately fainted after Billy dropped his bombshell. She was a very good fainter, and fainted on every major occasion in her life, apart from her own birth. (But then again, how do you know if a baby has fainted when it can't stand up to fall down?) After Dad picked her up from the kitchen floor, they grabbed each other and screamed at the ceiling. Buster took fright and ran out the back door. Then they calmed down a bit and went in search of Billy. He had wedged his head between the bed and the wardrobe when he was trying to hide so he was glad to see their feet in the bedroom doorway.

'Why on earth is Queen Alicia coming to 10 Rockfort Avenue?' Mum asked reasonably, after they had dislodged Billy's head.

'The lady servant woman said Her Majesty was a brilliant finder of lost things. She found her crown down the back of the sofa once after all 797 palace staff had given up the search. When she was a child she even found a bedroom in the castle that her parents had completely forgotten about.'

'I suppose it wouldn't be hard to forget about one bedroom when you have 689 rooms in the house,' Dad said. 'Anyway, there's no point in her coming because we searched the house from top to bottom and it's not here. The medal isn't going to magically reappear because the Queen is looking for it.'

'I'm not telling her not to come,' said Billy.

'I'm not telling her not to come,' said Mum.

And they looked at Dad for a long time. 'Hmm,' he said. 'Sure what harm would it do having the Queen in the house? It's just like having a friend coming to stay, but 1000 times more stressful.'

And then he and Mum held each other's hands again, looked at the ceiling and screamed.

Buster had just trotted up the stairs after recovering from the last screaming episode. These screams were even louder, with a hint of a frantic cry thrown in by Mum, so he bolted down the stairs so fast that he fell head over heels down the last five steps.

After everyone had calmed down again, Dad said they must draw up a list of tasks. Lists were his favourite thing in the whole world.

1. Make a few more threats to kill Billy but don't actually do so.

2. Buy lots of fancy biscuits.

3. Remove six years of junk and the Christmas decorations from the spare room.

4. Hide the mug with the Queen's picture on it because it's not very flattering.

5. Book a few days off work in case she stays after the weekend.

6. Do an Internet search to find out what the Queen likes to eat.

7.   Patch up the hole in the sitting room ceiling.

8.   Get fancy bathmats.

9.   Ask Gran to bake industrial quantities of her best apple tarts.

10. Tell nobody – repeat – nobody. Not even Gran. Especially not Gran.

Then Mum's email pinged on her phone. It was Gwendoline Penelope Remmington-Bakhurst with a series of instructions on hosting the Queen. Mum started to print out the list. After 24 pages, the printer ran out of paper. After 37 pages, the printer finally grew silent.

Mum and Dad looked at each other with crazed panic. Billy felt very bad indeed. This was all his fault. Then the phone pinged again. It was Gwendoline Penelope Remmington-Bakhurst with another set of instructions. She had made a mistake. The first set was only for public events.

Mum printed out the second set of instructions. The printer stopped after one page. She looked at the page. There were only three things written on it.

1. Her Majesty loves a nice slice of homemade apple tart every now and then.

2. Her Majesty enjoys an occasional chocolate biscuit.

3. Don't go to any trouble for her – really, I mean it. NO TROUBLE.

Of course, Mum and Dad completely ignored the last instruction, despite the important capital letters. They did not go to bed at all that night. Dad painted the spare room, landing and bathroom and replaced the missing tiles on the roof. Mum used the credit card so much in the home furnishings shop that it started to melt at the edges. And the cupboard door would not close because of the 65 packets of chocolate biscuits Mum had crammed in.

Gran enrolled three friends to peel apples for her as she started into an apple-tart baking marathon. They thought it was for a school fair.

Billy finally went to sleep at 4 AM to the sound of Dad hammering down the new carpet in the spare room. He heard a strange noise at 6 AM and awoke to see Dad on a ladder outside, washing the windows. When he went into the bathroom at 7 AM, Mum was re-grouting the tiles.

At 9 AM, the doorbell rang. Gran was on the doorstep, accompanied by 13 apple tarts on a trolley, some still warm.

She tried to come into the house but Dad blocked her because Gran was the best detective ever and would immediately grow suspicious if she saw the home improvements. She was already wondering why a school fair was being held during the summer holidays. Dad stepped out of the house and quickly closed the door behind him. But before he did, Gran saw Billy standing in the kitchen eating porridge in a three-piece suit.

Hmm, she said to herself. *That's quite suspicious.*

Dad walked Gran back to her car, half lifting her as they approached the car to speed her up. She wasn't a bit happy about this because she had expected to have a nice cup of tea and a slice of tart as a reward for all her hard work. Then Mum came down the street looking like she had just walked out of a hair salon, which she had. It had taken 34 phone calls to get a hairdresser to open up early for her but the curly bounce in her hair made it all worth it.

Gran's radar for suspicious activity started to ping like crazy. Her radar never let her down. It pinged when Billy started to feed pepperoni to the guinea pig. It pinged when he was in the middle of painting Buster white with black spots so that he would look like a Dalmatian. And it pinged non-stop when he offered her pâté on crackers, but it turned out to be Buster's dog food.

Yes, nothing got past Gran, perhaps because she was a recovering spy. She had been the country's top spy but her doctor ordered her to give it up after she had a heart attack. Still, every now and then she couldn't help herself and she would disappear for a few days to do a spot of spying. This suspicious activity at 10 Rockfort Avenue was just what she needed to sink her teeth into as things had been a bit quiet on the spying front recently.

Magnolia paint in Benjy's hair. Billy eating porridge in a three-piece suit. Brenda's hair looking suspiciously bouncy. Hmmm, I'll get to the bottom of this riddle or my name isn't Violet Bushell. Then she remembered her name wasn't actually Violet Bushell. That was just an alias she had used for her last spying job. *Whatever, I'll still get to the bottom of this,* she said to herself as she hopped into her car.

Gran shot off down the street just before a long black car swooped into view behind her and came to a silent stop outside the house.

Dad was surprised to find that the Queen wasn't in the car. Nor the lady servant. A man in a peaked cap got out and wheeled a gold suitcase to the doorstep. They both stood and looked at the suitcase in silence. For a crazy moment, Dad wondered if the Queen was about to jump out of it. He didn't know if his heart could withstand that kind of excitement. 'Her Majesty is probably in your back garden,' he told Dad in response to the questioning look on his face. 'She doesn't want to attract attention.'

Dad and the driver ran through the house and out the back just in time to see a crown being thrown over the fence into the garden. Then an elegant hand in a lace glove appeared over the fence, followed by a foot in a diamond-encrusted shoe. There was a loud crash and there she was. Queen Alicia was lying in the garden, looking like she might have broken several bones.

The lady servant came hurtling over the fence behind her and fell on top of the Queen.

'This is not a good start to proceedings,' said Mum, biting her lip and curtsying like crazy.

But, miraculously, the Queen hopped up, dusted herself off and declared: 'That was the best fun one has had in years. Wonderful sport.'

Gwendoline Penelope Remmington-Bakhurst did not look as pleased but she eventually got back on her feet and handed the crown to the Queen.

Mum ushered them into the kitchen, where Billy was standing, a lump of porridge stuck to the lapel of his suit.

'My darling boy,' said the Queen, hugging him tight and getting porridge on her gold-embroidered dress. 'One has answered your call of distress and come to help you in your hour of need. If that medal is in this house one will find it. And perhaps when this is all over we can do some maths together. One really wants to learn all about trigonometry.'

Billy was still reeling with the shock of seeing the Queen vaulting over the garden fence. Now here she was standing in their kitchen with porridge on her dress. It was the strangest thing that had ever happened to him. Well, one of the strangest things, if you include the time he was doing sums in her bedroom at 4.12 AM.

He remembered his manners and bowed to her. Unfortunately, Dad had decided to bow at exactly the same time and their heads cracked together like two eggs. By the time they had recovered, the lady servant and driver had left and it was just the Queen and the Browns sitting at the kitchen table eating apple tart and fancy chocolate biscuits. They were amazed that the Queen did not have any bodyguards or servants with her. In fact, Mum had run out after the lady servant to ask if she was not staying but she just said it was better this way.

'Suppose someone tries to kidnap her?' Mum asked.

'My dear,' said Gwendoline Penelope Remmington-Bakhurst, 'who, in their right mind, would think that the Queen would be staying in an incredibly small and modest semi-detached house on Rockfort Avenue? She's probably safer here than in the palace. None the less, our driver Constantine Sebastien Wolfenburg-Mannerheim will be staying locally and has arranged the rental of a discreet ten-year-old car so that he can drive around every hour on the hour and surreptitiously check in on Her Majesty.'

'Very good,' said Mum, who was slightly annoyed to hear her house described as tiny, but didn't let it show. 'Can I ask just one more thing? Is it mandatory to have at least one double-barrelled name to work in the palace?'

'Well, if you have two double-barrelled names it is more impressive on your CV but one double-barrelled name will guarantee you a job interview,' said Gwendoline Penelope Remmington-Bakhurst.

And, with that, the two people with extremely long names left the Queen in the company of the four people with very short names.

After tea, Mum showed the Queen to the spare room and asked Billy to hang around on the landing in case she needed anything.

He felt a bit awkward loitering outside the door and was just deciding to leave when he heard a squeaking noise and giggling. The door was slightly ajar and Billy peeked in. The Queen was jumping up and down on the bed with a big smile on her face. Then she spotted Billy and immediately stopped.

'One does apologise,' she said. 'It's just that one cannot jump on one's bed in the palace because there are too many servants around.'

Billy completely understood. He could never steal biscuits in the kitchen because there were too many people around. 'Try the other bed, Your Lady Highness,' he said. It's much bouncier.'

And so it was. Billy bounced on one bed. The Queen bounced on the other and Mum and Dad scratched their heads downstairs as they listened to the laughter.

7

Billy and the Queen were getting on like a house on fire. So much so that Dad had to call them five times when lunch was ready.

'One is frightfully sorry,' said Queen Alicia as she ran down the stairs. 'Appalling manners on my part. Billy was showing one his Lego collection and one simply could not drag oneself away. Now, how does lunch proceed in your lovely home?'

'Well,' said Dad, 'we just sit at the table and eat it.'

'How simply wonderful!' said the Queen, clasping her hands to her cheeks. 'No trumpet fanfare to announce your arrival? No servants standing at your shoulder to lift the silver cloche from your plate? No string quartet playing melodious music at a discreet distance? This is rather splendid.'

Mum and Dad had prepared a lovely smoked salmon salad but now it seemed very lacklustre without a blast of music from an orchestra. For the first time in her life, Mum found herself wishing she had learned how to play the trumpet instead of the stupid tin whistle. For the first time in his life, Dad found himself wondering if any shop on the high street stocked those silver cloches. And for the first time in his life, Billy wondered if he could force himself to eat lettuce. Normally his parents wouldn't even bother putting salad on his plate but it was clear that Mum and Dad were using the Queen's visit to force him to start eating green things. How low could they go?

But Billy could go lower.

'Is it true that you employ someone to chew your food, Your Royal Ladyship?' Billy asked.

Mum and Dad both dropped their cutlery with a crash at exactly the same moment.

The Queen looked surprised and then a big smile stretched across her face as she watched

Dad's face going a strange shade of purple. 'Is that what my subjects really think?'

'No, no, no, no, no,' said Mum and Dad at the same time.

'Well,' said Billy, looking straight at Dad, 'when we were planning the meals, you said the Queen would probably bring someone along to chew her food.'

Benjy went bright red and started stammering and stuttering until the Queen raised her gloved hand.

'No need to explain, my dear. One understands you were making a poor attempt at being humorous, albeit at one's expense. One expects one shall find the comedy in it when one has had time to reflect on it at a later stage.'

And then she winked at Mum, who laughed into her napkin and said to herself: *I'm sharing a private joke with the Queen. My life cannot possibly get any better.*

Dad gave Billy a good kick under the table but Billy didn't notice, as he was too busy wondering why the Queen had not mentioned the medal once since she arrived. He thought she was coming to find the thing but now it looked like she just wanted to eat large amounts of apple tart and bounce on the bed.

Mum was also wondering if she should mention the medal. And she would like to ask when the Queen was going home because there was a chance they might run out of fancy biscuits and Gran's apple tarts. They were already starting the second tart and there were only 11 more left.

'Make the tea, Benjy,' said Mum, in an attempt to move the conversation on from royal food chewers.

'One would like to help,' said the Queen, standing up. 'Where do you store your fine bone china?'

Luckily Mum and Dad had received a set of china cups and saucers as a wedding present and had taken them out of the attic at 3 AM. Mum wasn't sure if it was fine bone china, or just china but it was the best thing they had to offer.

But before she could show the Queen where they were, Her Majesty was opening the cupboard under the sink. There she found Mum's royal mug, which Dad had hidden – very badly, by the way.

'Is that one's face?' the Queen said, holding the mug aloft.

The mug should never have been put in the dishwasher but of course it had been, and so the picture of the Queen had started to disintegrate. Her beautiful luxuriant hair had worn away and her face had turned a peculiar shade of green. It was most unflattering.

But the Queen was thrilled. 'One adores this,' she declared. 'Is there even a slight possibility that you would part with this fascinating object? My lady servant would ensure that you were paid handsomely for it.'

'Not only that,' said Dad, 'but you can have your tea in it right now.' And so they sat around the table like four old friends, laughing and talking until Mum's forehead started to throb after the eighth cup of tea.

'What would you like to do now?' she asked the Queen, fully expecting her to say they should start the search for the medal.

Instead, the Queen asked if she could help with the household tasks. Billy escaped to kick football in the garden and Mum introduced the Queen to the washing machine. She was so fascinated by it that she pulled up a chair to watch the clothes whirling around. However, she had to stop looking after a few minutes because she felt sea-sick.

'One needs some air,' she said. 'Do you have any mundane errands one could assist with? Do you have to inspect the horses or look at the gardener's plans for the next season?'

'Your Highness mustn't have noticed that our garden is the size of a postage stamp and it definitely doesn't have room for a pony,' said Dad, 'but we do have to go to the bottle bank.'

The Queen thought it was an actual bank that converted bottles into money but when she heard that you got to throw bottles into a big drum she got very excited.

Mum said it didn't seem appropriate to bring Her Majesty to a bottle bank.

'Nonsense,' she said. 'One makes so many speeches about the environment and the need to recycle yet one has never attended a bank for bottles.' But then she looked down at her gold-embroidered dress, lace gloves and dia-mond-encrusted shoes. 'Should one put on a

more appropriate ensemble when one is recycling glass?'

That was a good idea. She was far too recognisable. Perhaps people would walk past her at the bottle bank if she was dressed like an ordinary person. Of course, the Queen had no idea what clothes had been packed for her because the lady servant had done the packing. Mum opened her suitcase to discover that the Queen had two tiaras, a spare crown, three evening gowns, a silk dress and a pair of green wellingtons.

Mum was delighted to see that she had also packed the fabulously ornate pink cashmere dressing gown, nightdress and gold slippers. She put the gold toothbrush in the glass beside her own and made a mental note to take a photo of it later.

Then Mum brought the Queen into her own bedroom and asked if she wanted to borrow a pair of shorts and a T-shirt. After all it was very hot between the rain showers, and they were all sweating in the fancy clothes they had put on for the Queen. Now that she seemed like a very relaxed type of queen, Mum thought they could get back into their shorts again.

The Queen's eyes were as big as saucers when Mum held up a pair of white shorts. 'One has not worn shorts since one was three years old,' she said. 'One didn't realise that they make shorts for adults. What a liberating and marvellous idea! One hopes one is not speaking too soon, but this day is shaping up to be the best day in one's life.' And before Mum could say anything, the Queen was trying to unzip her gold-embroidered dress.

8

The trip to the bottle bank was a great success. The Queen was unrecognisable in her ordinary-person's disguise of flip-flops, shorts and T-shirt. Dad had to suggest that she remove the crown, tie up her hair and put on a peaked cap before they left the house.

The Queen broke the first bottle she put into the bottle bank and she looked crestfallen. 'Is it no good for recycling now?' she asked Dad. On hearing that it didn't matter if they broke, she was overjoyed, and she and Billy competed with each other to see who could smash the most bottles.

A few people looked at the pony-tailed woman in shorts and thought she looked vaguely familiar. They came to the conclusion that she looked like the woman on the television ad for gravy granules but decided against

asking for a selfie because they weren't 100 per cent sure.

Meanwhile, Mum took advantage of their absence to try on the Queen's dressing gown and slippers and stalk around the house fanning herself with an imaginary fan and talking in an extremely posh voice.

The Queen wanted to do more jobs after the bottle bank so Dad brought her to the garage to get a tyre pumped up.

'You look fierce like the woman off the gravy granules ad,' said the mechanic to the Queen, who blushed and turned her head away.

Dad could see the Queen was enjoying wandering around like an ordinary person so he took her to the post office, the fruit and vegetable shop and the library.

'One has been in many libraries,' she whispered, 'but one has never been allowed to look at the books. This is exhilarating.'

And off she trotted with Billy to see if there were any books about her in the royal section. They found 28. Billy took out 12 on his library card but warned her that she couldn't take any of them back to the palace with her or he would be fined 10 cent a week for every missing one.

The librarian looked at the Queen as she checked out the books. 'Did anyone ever tell you –' she began to say, but the Queen cut her off.

'That one looks like the lady on the gravy granules ad? All the time.'

Billy froze. Would the librarian recognise the Queen's voice? Especially that weird way she always said 'one' instead of 'I'? But she continued to scan the books and said nothing more. Phew, that was close.

'You maybe should not talk to anyone when you are in your ordinary-person disguise,' Billy said as they walked back to the car. 'You do have a very, very posh voice.'

'One has never thought so,' the Queen said. 'When one meets people at events, they always sound the same as oneself. Perhaps one's accent is contagious? When one leaves your home, perhaps you too will speak as though you have two boiled eggs lodged in your mouth.'

And then she just burst into tears. Billy didn't know what to do. Dad was even more frazzled when she got into the car crying.

'What did you do to her?' he hissed at Billy as he searched for a tissue in the glove compartment.

'The poor child did nothing wrong. It was just the thought of leaving your wonderful home that made one quite emotional,' the Queen said, blowing her nose as loudly as a trumpet. 'One is having such a nice time with your family that one does not want it to end.'

Heavens above, said Dad to himself. *We'll never get rid of this woman, nice and all as she is.*

The Queen was in bed at 8 PM that night after the excitement of the day, and everyone else was in bed at 8.01 PM. The Brown family had discovered that entertaining royalty was exhausting, even when they were as nice as the Queen.

Mum remembered how the Queen said she awoke at 4 AM every morning, so Mum got up at 3.30 on Sunday morning to prepare some boiled eggs. However, 4 AM passed and there was no sound from upstairs. Then 5 AM. Eventually Mum awoke at 9 AM, her face stuck to the kitchen table.

To her delight, the Queen had come downstairs in her regal dressing gown and gold slippers.

'One has had the most delightful sleep of one's entire life,' she said. 'Who knew one could sleep for so long when one is not awoken by the servant of the servant of the lady servant?'

It was another busy day for the Queen, as she wanted to help out with all the household tasks. She put out the rubbish – 'most satisfactory'. She fed Buster – 'most entertaining' – and she hung up clothes on the line – 'most educational'. Dad caught Billy trying to get the Queen to clean up the dog's poo in the garden and gave him a good telling-off but, other than that, everything went amazingly well. That was until Gran almost triggered a national security alert.

They were all sitting around the table eating roast chicken and the Queen was excitedly recalling how she had licked her first ever stamp with her face on it when they went to the post office the previous day. Then she looked straight ahead and froze. They all turned to see what had stopped the Queen in her tracks. It was someone wearing a balaclava and dressed entirely in black and he was abseiling past the kitchen window.

'Suffering ducks,' said Dad. This was his favourite expression of shock and made absolutely no sense.

'I'll be a monkey's uncle,' said Mum, which made even less sense, if that was possible. They were all frozen to the spot.

Then the Queen gave a polite cough. 'One is growing slightly anxious that one will be kidnapped,' she said in a low voice.

Dad sprang into action, bolting out through the patio door. He didn't know what he would do to the intruder when he got outside and there was nothing but blind panic in his mind, but he knew he should be doing something. At the same time Mum picked up the phone and started to dial.

Then she heard a familiar voice. 'It's only me, dears.' The man in the balaclava who had arrived to kidnap the Queen was actually only Gran.

'What the hell are you doing, Mother?' asked Mum, rushing to the door. 'We thought we were all going to be assassinated.'

'I'm on a mission to uncover your secret and I have done so,' said Gran triumphantly. 'Who's that woman eating roast chicken in your kitchen? Oh, she's not there now.' They all turned to look. Where had the Queen gone?

Mum and Dad rushed inside to find Billy pushing the Queen's bottom into the little cupboard under the stairs before slamming it shut.

'It's OK,' said Dad. 'You can let her out.'

The Queen reversed out of the cupboard in as dignified a way as possible when you are crawling out of a tiny cupboard backwards. She straightened up to face Gran.

'Why is the woman from the gravy granules ad trying to hide in your cupboard?' Gran asked. 'This is not what I expected at all, at all.'

The Queen smiled at her. 'One really must see this advertisement you all speak of so glowingly.'

It was Gran's turn to freeze. 'Goodness gracious me,' she declared. 'It's the Queen,' and she

fanned herself. 'I really don't feel very well,' she said, before fainting in a heap. (This is where Mum got her fainting habit from.)

Mum was extremely cross with Gran but she had to hold on to her crossness until Gran woke up from her fainting fit. 'Why on earth did you abseil down the side of the house? Why not just ring the front door like a normal grandmother?' she asked.

Gran said she wanted the element of surprise. 'And I love dressing up in my old spy clothes and abseiling down buildings. Aah,' she said, with longing in her voice, 'I miss those crazy days.'

The Queen was fascinated by Gran and wanted to hear all about her spying days, so they went back to the kitchen table to finish dinner. And when the Queen heard Gran was the chief apple-tart maker, she warmed to her even more. They discovered they were born on the same day and shared the same unnatural but terrifying fear of clowns. They both loved ginger biscuits and hated banoffee pie.

After a while, Mum, Dad and Billy left them in the kitchen and had a mini-conference in the sitting room.

'Queen Alicia is great, isn't she?' said Billy. Mum and Dad smiled and agreed.

'So much fun,' said Mum.

'So easy-going,' said Dad.

And they looked at each other, waiting for someone to say it.

'But when do you think she's going home?' Billy said finally. 'We have only 62 packets of biscuits left.'

'Exactly,' said Mum and Dad at the same time.

'We've done no searching for the medal at all,' said Dad. 'I can't help but think that she has no interest in finding it.'

'But why is she here then?' asked Billy. 'Maybe they are making some sort of reality show about the Queen with hidden cameras? Maybe we are the stars? Maybe we are really famous in the outside world right now.'

10

They all thought about the idea of living in a reality show for a moment. Mum remembered prancing around the house in the Queen's dressing gown and she really hoped Billy's theory was wrong.

Dad also hoped that Billy was wrong because he had snuck downstairs last night and eaten half a packet of biscuits when everyone was in bed. Could the cameras have caught that?

Billy was quite excited at the idea of being a reality television star but he really hoped the cameras didn't catch him pretending to be James Bond in the bathroom mirror.

Then he remembered how Gwendoline Penelope Remmington-Bakhurst had gone upstairs to help the Queen settle in and wondered if she had planted hidden cameras everywhere.

Just then Gran burst into the sitting room. 'Can I stay the night? The Queen has a spare bed in her room and she's never had anyone for a sleepover, ever. Please, please, please say yes. It's not a school night.'

Mum and Dad often complained about Billy's sleepovers because the children stayed up talking until approximately 3 AM and popcorn turned up in the most unusual places afterwards (up Billy's nose, for example). Well, if they thought Billy's friends were bad, Gran and the Queen were ten times worse. Even Billy asked them to keep the noise down after they went trampolining at 4.30 AM. That was even noisier than the rollerblading at midnight. At 6 AM they awoke to hear Gran making pancakes.

It seemed that Gran and the Queen had become firm friends. After eating a massive plate of pancakes, they went back to bed for a few hours and then Gran brought the Queen to her house to show her where great apple tarts were made. As he watched Gran and the Queen accelerating down the road at an alarming speed in Gran's tiny car, Billy wondered if he should be jealous. After all, the Queen was his friend first. Was Gran stealing her away from Billy? But when he thought about it, he realised he didn't feel even a tiny bit cross. In fact, he was proud that the Queen liked Gran so much. Billy knew that she was the world's coolest granny and the universe's top apple-tart maker but not many other people knew that. It was only right that that the empire's most important person had a chance to discover just how great she was.

Gran had a second sleepover that night, but this time both women were in bed at 8 PM. Everyone else followed at 8.01 PM as they hadn't got a wink of sleep the night before.

When Billy came into the kitchen the next morning, Gran was taking hot scones out of the oven and Mum and Dad were sitting at the table licking their lips.

'Mm-mm,' said Billy, grabbing one, but Gran ran him out of the kitchen. 'Go in and entertain Alicia,' she told him. 'I must talk to your parents.'

'Who?' said Billy. No one had ever heard the Queen referred to by her first name only before. It felt very strange. Yet Gran had said it like she had known the Queen forever. Billy was getting prouder of Gran with every moment that passed.

He took the Queen up to his room to play with his Lego while Gran brought Mum and Dad up to date with the visit. Gran's spy senses had kicked in and she was very suspicious.

'She is not here to help you search for the medal,' she said. 'She has an ulterior motive, and I think I know what it is.'

'What, what?' demanded Mum and Dad.

'She just wants to be with you lot – don't ask me why. A more boring suburban family you couldn't find. But there you go.'

'You're calling us boring?' said Billy, who had just crept into the kitchen to see if there were any scones left. 'Us? Boring? Remember when I got my head stuck in the banister and

Dad had to cut the stairs with a chainsaw to release me. I thought that was pretty exciting.'

Mum nodded. 'And what about the time I forgot to put the handbrake on and the car rolled down the street and crashed into four parked cars, a lorry-load of bananas and a Ferris wheel? That was the most excitement the neighbourhood had seen in at least 10 years. It was on the front page of the *Rockfort Gazette*, for heaven's sake.'

'Okay, okay,' said Gran, holding up her hands. 'You are a tiny percentage more exciting than the average family, but that's not the point.' Gran explained how the Queen just wanted to live with a normal family and do normal things. 'She hasn't stopped banging on about how marvellous it is to be treated as part of a family and how stacking the dishwasher gives her a greater sense of satisfaction than a royal visit to Kyrgyzstan. Or was it Kazakhstan? I'm not entirely sure.'

'Whether it was Kyrgyzstan or Kazakhstan isn't important right now,' said Dad. 'Although

I see your problem. I often get those two countries mixed up. I also confuse Mauritania and Mauritius on a regular basis, even though geographically they are nowhere near each other, unlike Kyrgyzstan and Kazakhstan.'

'Don't even get me started on Turkmenistan and Tajikistan,' said Mum. 'Or Uzbekistan and Uruguay.'

'Stop right now!' shouted Gran. 'We are going off on a tangent. Back to Her Majesty, please. Anyway, all she wants is a normal, boring life like you lot have. I'll never understand people. She's still going on about the wonder of shorts for adults, for goodness' sake. And the joy of bouncing on a bed. She has no life at all in that palace. It's like a prison. A very fancy prison where everything is slathered in gold, but a prison all the same.'

Suddenly it all made sense. Billy immediately felt sorry for the Queen. Mum and Dad wondered if this meant that she would never go home, ever.

Gran had more pressing things on her mind.

'I bet you the disappearance of the medal is linked with Alicia. I bet she ordered that it be stolen so that she could come here. I bet if you searched her fancy luggage you would find that medal.'

Mum and Dad couldn't believe what they were hearing. Could Her Majesty really have orchestrated the disappearance of the medal?

'No offence to the Queen,' said Dad, 'but I don't think she has the type of brain that could plan something like that.'

'I agree,' said Billy. 'Remember how it took her 15 minutes to figure out how to put on a pair of flip-flops? I don't think she is as cunning as you imagine.'

'We'll soon find out,' said Gran, and she vaulted across the kitchen chair for no particular reason at all. 'I'm going to search her luggage while you all distract her.'

11

Mum and Dad charged to stop her but they both got stuck in the doorway as Gran leaped up the stairs, taking two steps at a time. She was surprisingly agile for a 59-year-old woman.

She met Her Majesty at the top of the stairs. The Queen had tired of Billy's Lego collection and wanted to try the swing ball set in the back garden.

Excellent, said Gran to herself. *If Brenda plays with her, that will give me approximately seven minutes and 23 seconds to search for the medal.*

Gran had remembered that when Billy's mother was young, she always got hit in the head by the swing ball about seven minutes into the game. Gran added on 23 seconds in case Brenda would be too polite to stop the game immediately.

As soon as the Queen and Brenda went into the garden, Gran put on her tight black spying gloves and entered the spare room. The gold suitcase was under the bed but it gave up no secrets. Tiaras, green wellingtons and evening dresses were lovely but they were no good for Gran's mission. Suddenly the door swung open. Gran's heart stopped for three milliseconds. But it was only Billy. Phew.

'I want to help you on your mission,' Billy whispered, even though there was no way the Queen would hear him.

'Good, but why are you wearing a black ski-mask and your mother's pink fluffy slippers?' Gran whispered back.

'Fail to prepare, prepare to fail,' Billy whispered in a mysterious fashion. 'Now, did you search the locker?'

They both looked at the bedside locker. There was a picture of the King in a gold frame. *Aah*, said Gran to herself. *I had forgotten about the King.* And she immediately felt sorry for the Queen. The King had died exactly one week after the royal couple got married, many, many years ago. It was a very sad time for the country because everyone thought they were a perfect match.

Gran's husband had died ten years ago and she remembered how lonely she had felt. She still felt lonely sometimes, even though she had a lot of friends and family to talk to. What must it be like to be locked away in a palace with no one to talk to except servants?

'I wonder if Alicia Hildegard Alexandra von Fuffenburg has any true friend?' Gran said to Billy.

'One doesn't think the head of an empire is allowed to have friends,' said a voice behind them. The Queen had come in to change into Mum's sneakers because she fell out of her flip-flops and hit Mum in the face with her racket.

Seven minutes and 45 seconds, Gran noted, looking at her stopwatch. *Well done, Brenda!*

'That's nonsense,' said Gran. 'You are the leader of the empire so if you want to have friends you can have them. Don't heed any stupid rule book for royalty. Everyone needs friends. Even queens. Especially queens.'

And she gave the Queen a big hug without even thinking about the 'no touching' rule. The Queen obviously didn't mind because she hugged her back.

'Let's be friends so,' said the Queen. 'We can have joint birthday parties. But first you'll have to talk me through the protocols. This is all new to me.'

'I have just three rules,' said Gran.

'1. We must never do anything that involves clowns because they are obviously evil and terrifying.

'2. It is mandatory to go rollerblading once a week.

'3. You must make it a criminal offence to serve banoffee pie in public from now on.'

The Queen clapped her hands with delight. 'One loves your rules. Can one add another rule? 4. Apple tart must be consumed on all friend-type activities. And now, what are you and Billy doing in my bedroom?' she asked.

Gran immediately blushed and Billy realised the ski-mask was not the brilliant disguise he thought it was. How were they going to explain this? Gran decided to share the blame.

'It was all Billy's fault,' she said, feeling slightly guilty at blaming an innocent nine-year-old boy. 'He grew suspicious about your lack of interest in finding the medal and then he thought that perhaps you had ordered someone to take the medal so that you could get away from the palace for a few days and live with your subjects. We were just searching your luggage to see if you had the medal, because that would back up his theory.'

But as soon as she said it she knew that the theory was wrong because Her Majesty looked totally mystified. Billy kept opening and closing his mouth like a fish. He couldn't decide who he was more afraid of angering — the Queen or Gran.

'If only one had a devious and cunning mind like you suggest,' said the Queen. 'One would be able to take over empires all over the world and make them one's own.' Her eyes grew wide at the idea. 'One would be able to follow summer around the world. One could have one's own pet camel named Humphry. One could pick fruit from the trees for breakfast. One might never live in this empire again,' she said, looking out the window at the lashing rain.

Gran snapped her fingers. 'You must focus, Al – I can shorten your name now that we are friends. Do you like Al, or Ali?'

The Queen thought for a moment. 'You can call me Al,' she declared with a regal tone in her voice and then she shook her shoulders with delight. 'It's stupendously exciting to finally get a nickname when one is aged 59.'

Gran snapped her fingers again. 'Focus, Al. How do we explain the missing medal?'

The Queen thought for another moment. 'Ali does have a nice ring to it too. Hmmm. But back to business. The only person I know with a cunning and devious mind like that is Gwendoline Penelope Remmington-Bakhurst.'

They all looked at each other with their mouths open. Could the very polite and well-spoken lady servant have cooked up such a dastardly plan? And why?

'What should one do if this is true?' the Queen asked Gran and Billy. 'Does the empire still behead people? Should one send her to the gallows? Or the dungeons? Do we even have dungeons anymore? One is really out of touch with palace affairs. Please bring me my gold-plated telephone so that I can summon her.'

Now that the Queen was annoyed with someone else, Billy thought it would be a perfect moment to make a confession. His offence would seem very small beside Gwendoline's scheming plan.

'I am extremely sorry, Your Royalness,' he said to the Queen as he lifted her mattress to reveal half a packet of very soggy frozen peas.

'So that explains the pea smell,' said Gran. 'I thought it was Al's feet and I didn't want to say anything because it's a criminal offence to accuse a Queen of having smelly feet.'

'After the Queen arrived,' Billy explained, 'I thought it would be fun to do the test where you put a pea under the mattress to see if the princess is really a princess. But because I like the Queen very, very much I slipped in approximately 87 peas, to give her a good chance of finding them.'

'First of all,' said Queen Alicia, 'that only works with princesses and I am a queen as you know. Second of all, you really should use a dried pea. Third of all, I would recommend 12 mattresses, to ensure that the experiment is being conducted in a systematic and scientific manner. And fourth of all, I also smelled peas but I thought this is how a family home should smell so I said nothing. Now, get your parents. We must tell them about this devious plot we have uncovered and then we must summon Gwendoline Penelope Remmington-Bakhurst here immediately. There's a good chance she will be executed at dawn because of the conniving plan she has concocted.'

The Queen and Gran brought the Browns up to date with their theory about the missing medal and it all made perfect sense. That explained why the lady servant had spent so much time in the house that first day she had called to see them. She was obviously biding her time to steal the medal when no one was looking. But why?

'I have several theories,' declared Gran in an important voice, as she puffed out her chest. 'But my favourite theory is that she sold the medal in order to fund her escape from the palace. She is probably wearing a flower in her hair and sipping a cocktail out of a coconut shell on a beach in Mauritius right now. Or is it Mauritania? I get those two countries mixed up all the time. I wouldn't be surprised if she has already changed her name to Cristina Benedetta Maria Barberini-Ludovisi, just to deceive the authorities.'

'I like the way your mind works, my brand-new friend,' said the Queen. 'Would you agree

that execution by a firing squad is the correct punishment?'

'Not at all,' said Gran, looking at Billy's horrified face. 'Live and let live. Let her go in peace. She has been carrying around those four names for 40-something years. She needs a break. You don't really need all those servants anyway.'

Just then the doorbell rang and who was standing on the doorstep but the arch-criminal herself – Gwendoline Penelope Remmington-Bakhurst!

12

Billy felt a rush of wind behind him and before he knew it, Gran had dashed past him, wrestled the lady servant to the ground and was sitting spreadeagled on top of her.

'Finally we've captured you,' said Gran proudly, as though she had been searching all her life for the woman.

'Oh dear me, oh dear me,' Gwendoline Penelope Remmington-Bakhurst kept repeating. 'This is highly irregular.'

'Mother!' shouted Mum at Gran. 'Release that woman right now. She's probably a baroness or something.'

'Actually I'm just Lady Remmington-Bakhurst,' said the lady servant, dusting herself off after Gran stood up. 'I'm a very minor aristocrat. Now, how may I help you?'

Billy was feeling very left out after Gran's heroics so he launched into the theory that she was the medal thief and she was late for her appointment with a cocktail on a Mauritius beach.

'What an astute young boy!' Gwendoline Penelope Remmington-Bakhurst marvelled, while also secretly wondering why he was wearing a ski-mask and pink fluffy slippers. 'You are half right and half wrong. Yes, I did secrete the medal on my person on that fateful day I called to issue the invitation to the garden party. However, my reason was more altruistic than you have given me credit for.'

'Go on,' said Billy, making a mental note to look up the word 'altruistic' after she left.

'You see, when you called to the palace at 4.12 AM that morning to explain the mathematical conundrum, I saw a light in Ma'am's eyes that I had not seen in a very long time. She was positively glowing as she spent time with you. She never stopped talking about you after you left, but by lunchtime, the sadness had returned to her eyes. *If only I could make Ma'am happy again*, I thought. *If only she could spend more time with Billy*. Under what pretext could I invite you back to the palace, I wondered. It was then that I hatched the plan to bring Ma'am here under false pretences. The medal is perfectly safe, I can assure you. I had planned to reunite you with it when Her Majesty was ready to go home. By the way, I think you have a pea infestation in your home. The smell is very strong.'

Gwendoline Penelope Remmington-Bakhurst had been looking down at the ground as she made her little speech and now she looked up fearfully, wondering what her fate would be. 'I am prepared to take my punishment, Ma'am,' she said, holding out her wrists as though the Queen had a pair of handcuffs in her back pocket and was ready to slap them on.

But Queen Alicia wasn't furious at all. She had tears in her eyes. So had Mum and Dad, although Dad later said it was just a bit of dust.

'My darling Gwendoline,' said the Queen, giving her a warm hug. 'That is the kindest thing anyone has ever done for me. One should make you a duchess for services rendered to the royal household.'

The only one who was not happy was Gran. She looked deflated because she no longer had a master criminal to track down. She went into the kitchen to make tea and they all trooped after her.

It emerged that Gwendoline Penelope Remmington-Bakhurst had not come to confess about the medal. There was something more pressing.

'Your people need you, Your Majesty,' she told the Queen. 'It's been four days since you've made a public appearance and people are asking questions. Look,' she said dramatically, and she turned on the little television on the kitchen counter. Everyone stared, wondering why they were looking at a kids' cartoon. She flicked the remote control and the gravy granules advertisement came on.

'Aah,' said Queen Alicia. 'One does see the resemblance.'

Lady Gwendoline flicked through more channels until she came to the breaking news service. A reporter was standing outside the palace and the caption read *Where is our beloved Queen Alicia?* Underneath the caption ran a news tickertape declaring: *Cucumber growers in crisis as uncertainty hangs over Queen's appearance at cucumber convention.*

'Oh, the competition to find the empire's longest cucumber!' exclaimed the Queen. 'One has presented the prize every year since one became Queen. The growers will be devastated if the palace is not represented. The entire cucumber industry could collapse with the shock. When is it on?'

'Tomorrow, Your Majesty,' said Gwendoline Penelope Remmington-Bakhurst. 'Regrettably you have also missed another personal favourite – the ugliest pet in the empire competition. A one-legged, three-eyed hairless cat won it this year. It was very controversial

as everyone thought the toothless dog with arthritis and oozing sores would take the crown.'

'Oh heavens,' said Her Majesty again. 'In one's excitement at living with the marvellous Brown family, one quite forgot about one's royal duties. Yes, one has been exceedingly negligent.'

I think this means the Queen wants to go home, said Billy to himself. *I'll kind of miss her. But at least I'll get my medal back.*

Gran looked even more deflated when she started to think about the Queen's return to the palace. She was just getting used to having a good friend and now they would be separated.

'Why not have one last night here and return in the morning to judge the cucumbers?' she suggested. 'After all, those scones aren't going to eat themselves.'

And so it was settled. The Queen would return to the palace in the morning and Billy would get his medal back.

After enjoying two very tasty scones with raspberry jam, Gwendoline Penelope Remmington-Bakhurst left and Gran took the Queen shopping for shorts. She bought six pairs and declared that she would wear them around the palace for ever more.

Mum and Dad were exhausted cooking fancy dinners for royalty so they decided to get a take-away for their last dinner with the Queen. She was thrilled and asked for pizza because she had only ever seen pictures of it in books. Gran left after that, with a promise that she would visit the Queen at least once a week and she would oversee the erection of a

14-foot trampoline with gold trimming in the Queen's private garden.

And then it was just the Queen and the Browns sitting around the kitchen table, eating apple tart. A quiet sadness descended on everyone as they thought about the Queen's departure. Saddest of all was the Queen, who tried not to show it because she had extremely good manners. She knew life would never be the same again, now that she had seen what it was like to load the dishwasher, hang clothes on the line and pick up dog poo. (Billy had finally succeeded in his attempt to get the Queen to clean up after Buster.)

But she also knew that her empire needed her and she had to do her duty, so she kept her chin high and didn't tell the Browns that her heart was slowly breaking inside. She put her gold-embroidered dress on a hanger in preparation for the morning and left her tiara on the bedside locker before going to bed. Except she didn't go to bed. When everyone was asleep, she crept out the door and into the darkness.

13

Mum and Dad awoke at 1 AM to hear Billy shouting, 'The Queen is gone! Someone stole the Queen! Help!'

He had been on his way to the toilet when he noticed the Queen's bedroom door was open. They all dashed into her room to find that her bed had not been slept in.

'Suffering ducks,' said Dad. 'This isn't good. This is very bad, in fact. It could be the worst thing that has ever happened to this family. We have lost the head of the empire. How careless is that?'

'Has she been kidnapped?' said Mum, running downstairs to see if there was any trace of a break-in. There wasn't. She had just vanished. 'Call Gran, now!' she shouted to Billy. 'I can't dial her number because my hands are shaking too much.' And then she fainted with the excitement of it all.

'Not again!' said Dad. 'Can we not have one good crisis in this house without someone collapsing into a heap?'

Gran was still wide awake when the phone rang. She couldn't sleep with worry as she thought about Queen Alicia rattling around in the lonely palace and trampolining alone with a very sad face.

As soon as Billy rang, she sprang into action and was at 10 Rockfort Avenue in three minutes, 43 seconds.

'Ah, Brenda, you're always losing things,' she said to Mum. 'First it was the medal, and now it's Alicia. What next? It's a good job your head is attached to your neck or you'd lose that too. Now, let's think,' she said. 'Where could she be? Was there any place she really liked going to?'

Billy remembered how excited the Queen was on the day she arrived, when they did all the mundane household tasks at the shops, garage, library and post office. But perhaps her favourite thing was the bottle bank. He ran out to the back door and saw the crate for the bottles was gone.

'Well, I never!' said Mum. 'Do you think the Queen really walked to the bottle bank with the crate under her oxter in the middle of the night?'

'There's only one way to find out,' said Gran. 'Follow me.' They all bundled into Gran's tiny car and sped down the road to the bottle bank. Billy was hoping the car wouldn't break down because he was wearing his Fireman Sam slippers. Mum was hoping the same because her nightdress was a bit see-through. Dad sat in the front seat, freezing in his boxer shorts and wondering why he wasn't the sort of man who wore pyjamas.

They pulled up at the bottle bank and heard the crash of a bottle.

'Wonderful,' tinkled Queen Alicia. 'That was the loudest noise yet.'

She was standing in her fabulous pearl-encrusted dressing gown and green wellingtons, flinging bottles into the drum. A sense of relief washed over everyone. Or was it just rain? The skies had opened and it was pouring.

'Let's get you into the car quickly, Your Majesty,' said Mum. 'I don't think that dressing gown is rain-proof.'

The Queen looked surprised to see Gran and the Browns standing there in their night clothes. She was particularly surprised by Dad's Superman boxer shorts and wondered if this was something all her male subjects wore. Then her lower lip started to wobble and she burst into tears.

'One had to return to the bottle bank one last time,' she said. 'One will miss this so very, very much,' and she dramatically hurled the last bottle into the drum and picked up the crate.

14

Billy had been watching all this and trying very hard to find a solution to the Queen's woes. She really was very lonely. Gran had turned out to be a good friend but now they would be separated. Gran was also a bit lonely and was missing all her spying work. Suddenly, Billy had the best idea of his whole life.

'Do you need a bodyguard by any chance, Your High Ladyship?' he asked the Queen. 'Because I know someone who would be perfect for that job.'

He looked at Gran.

Her Majesty looked at Gran.

Mum and Dad looked at Gran and back at the Queen.

This could be a marvellous solution for everyone. And it would mean that the Browns could visit the palace all the time.

'One knew you were a special boy when you walked into the royal bedroom at approximately 4.12 AM to solve that maths puzzle,' said the Queen. 'As it happens, one's head of security is retiring next month. And yes, your wonderful grandmother would be a marvellous replacement. One couldn't think of anyone one would feel safer with.

'Oh, but there is one problem,' she said, turning to Gran. 'What is your name?'

'Belinda Burton,' said Gran.

'No double-barrelled name lurking in there?' asked the Queen.

'Well,' said Gran. 'To be totally honest, my full married name was Belinda Mary Fitzpatrick Burton but I had a pain in my hand writing it so I dropped two names.'

'Splendid and excellent,' said the Queen, clapping her hands. 'You're hired. We are going to have such marvellous fun. We can spend every day together and go trampolining and apple-tart making in the evening. How wonderful is this? One's life will be transformed.

Now, can we go home please? One's pearls are starting to fall off one's dressing gown with this torrential rain and one has an exceedingly important cucumber competition to judge at noon.'

Gran decided to sleep over that night to ensure that the Queen didn't do any more roaming, but it was clear that she was going to bed happy. In fact, everyone was much happier going to bed, especially Mum who had just remembered the invitation to the Royal Garden Party and was mentally trying on outfits as she lay in bed.

She had finally settled on the correct pair of shoes to match her outfit when Gwendoline Penelope Remmington-Bakhurst rang the doorbell at 8 AM.

The lady servant was carrying the medal in its purple velvet case, as well as a smaller replica medal. 'Now you can put the big medal into the bank safe and keep the replica here,' she said.

Dad delighted the Queen by presenting her with the mug depicting her melted face.

He had also found one in the attic commemorating the King and Queen's marriage so she was absolutely thrilled. Mum presented an apple tart to Gwendoline Penelope Remmington-Bakhurst for coming up with such a devious but highly successful plan.

The Queen's chauffeur, Constantine Sebastien Wolfenburg-Mannerheim, had spent the past four days patrolling Rockfort Avenue in a modest ten-year-old car, hired for the purpose, as he surreptitiously kept an eye on the Queen, so he also deserved a gift but he declared that the experience was a gift in itself.

'I shall purchase a modest ten-year-old car as soon as I return to the palace,' he said.

'What a joy to drive! So easy to park. Can you imagine how hard it is to park a stretch limousine on the main street, or to find space at the filling station? Truly this experience has changed all our lives for the better. But if you really want to give me something, I've heard your apple tarts are legendary.'

One hour later, the Browns had waved off the Queen, Gran was on her way home to pack for her new job and all was well with the world again. 'Phew!' said Mum and Dad together as they closed the front door. 'That was some experience!'

Mum turned to Billy.

'Now, Billy, we'll hop into the car and take that medal to the bank for safe-keeping. Where is it?'

'I don't have it,' said Billy.

'I don't have it,' said Dad.

'Well, I certainly don't have it,' said Mum, and she winked at Dad.

'Oh, oh,' said Billy. 'Here we go again!'

And they all burst out laughing.

A Mathematical Note from Billy

I really find this hard to believe, but there are still a lot of people in this world who don't understand how dividing something by a fraction makes it bigger. Even adults keep saying: 'Explain the Queen's very, very tricky sum to me please.' I was quite surprised when the school principal called me into a quiet corner one day and asked me to explain it. Then he warned me that I must never speak of the conversation, ever, or I would be expelled. Oops.

But I'm glad that some people find it tricky because otherwise I would never have found myself in Queen Alicia's bedroom at approximately 4.12 AM. I wouldn't own the world's biggest, shiniest gold medal and I wouldn't be allowed to go rollerblading in the palace corridors every Sunday afternoon. The floors are so shiny and slippery. It's deadly. And I'm glad to say Gwendoline Penelope Remmington-Bakhurst will be out of hospital tomorrow. I didn't break her leg after all when I crashed into her. Only her ankle. Phew!

So, let's explain the Queen's very, very tricky sum for once and for all.

What are we really asking when we do a division sum? Take for example 10 divided by 2. We are asking how many 2s are in 10. The answer is 5.

Now, it's exactly the same with a fraction. Take for example 10 divided by ½.

We are asking how many halves are in 10. The answer is 20. (We do the sum by putting 10 over 1 and turning ½ upside-down and multiplying it, but perhaps that is too much information, too soon, for you.)

The smaller the fraction, the bigger the answer. So, 10 divided by ¼ is 40.

I hope that makes sense. If Queen Alicia understood it, then you definitely should.

Now, what about multiplying fractions? Ha, joking! That's quite enough mathematics for one day, as my good friend the Queen might say.

About the Author

Alison Healy has worked as a journalist with the *Irish Times* for almost 18 years. She specialises in food and farming issues but is currently on a career break, working as a ghost writer and on her children's fiction. This is her first children's book.

About the Illustrator

Fintan Taite is a freelance illustrator and cartoonist from Dublin. He is a member and former chairman of the Illustrators Guild of Ireland. His work has appeared in many newspapers and magazines in Ireland and abroad including *The Irish Times*, the *Sunday Tribune*, *Magill* and *The Dubliner*, and he has illustrated a number of books and advertising campaigns.

About the Publisher

Based in Dublin, Little Island Books has been publishing books for children and teenagers since 2010. It is Ireland's only English-language publisher that produces books exclusively for young people. Little Island specialises in new Irish writers and illustrators, and also has a commitment to publishing books in translation.